# Yo Ho! Let's Go!

adapted by Bill Scollon
illustrated by the Disney Storybook Artists

Reader's Digest
Children's Books®

New York, New York • Montréal, Québec • Bath, United Kingdom

It's a sunny day in Never Land. Skully is keeping watch over Pirate Island.

"Cheese and crackers!" he squawks. "All hands on beach!" Jake and his crew hurry out of the Hideout.

"What is it, Skully?" Jake yells.

"Something's washed ashore," answers the pirate parrot.

"It's an unidentified floating hat!" says Skully.

Jake looks it over. "I think I've seen this hat before," he says.

"Me, too," Izzy laughs. "On the head of a sneaky pirate captain!"

"Hook!" shouts Cubby. "He must have lost it."

"Well, we found it," says Jake. "So, it's up to us to return it!"

The crew is off to return Captain Hook's hat. Skully cries out, "Is everybody ready?"

"I've got my sword!" Jake replies.

"I've got my map," adds Cubby.

Izzy smiles. "And, I've got my Pixie Dust!" she says.

Along the way, the crew will solve Pirate Problems and collect Gold Doubloons!

"Ahoy! Do you want to join my pirate crew? Great! Put on your bandana and climb aboard! Yo ho, let's go!"

Aboard the Jolly Roger, Captain Hook is fuming! "Smee!" he bellows. "Where's my hat? I can't find it anywhere."

"Oh, dear," says Smee. "Don't worry, I have just the thing." Smee calls Sharky and Bones. "Bring out the hat rack!" he says.

"Here you are, sir," says Smee.
He puts a hat on the cranky captain.
"How about this one?" he asks.
"No!" says Hook.

"Okay, let's try this one."
"No!"

"This one is all the rage, sir."
"Enough!" yells Hook. "I
don't want just any hat. I want
my hat!"

Hook looks across the Never Sea.

"My hat must be out there somewhere," he says, grabbing his spyglass. "And, I'm going to find it!"

Hook sees Jake sailing toward him. He's wearing Hook's hat!

"Smee!" yells the captain. "That pesky Jake has stolen my hat!"

"Perhaps the sea pups found your hat," says Mr. Smee, "and they're returning it."

"Ridiculous!" scoffs Hook. "Hoist the anchor! We must get my hat!"

Smee and the crew snap to attention. "Right away, sir!" says Smee.

Hook's men run every which way as they ready the ship. In the commotion, Smee accidently knocks over Captain Hook!

"You clumsy oaf!" says Hook. The pirates rush to help their captain.

"Good thing the catapult broke your fall," Bones points out.

"Catapult?" asks Hook.

Suddenly, the catapult hurls Hook into the sky!

"Smeeee! Help me!" screams the captain. He flies over Jake and his crew and lands on an island.

Jake looks through his telescope. "I see him! Hook's stuck in a tree."

"He needs our help," says Izzy. "Let's go!" For finding Hook, the crew gets two Gold Doubloons!

The Never Land Pirates race to the island, but Hook's men are already there. "Get me down!" cries Hook.

"Yes, sir!" says Sharky. He shakes the tree, knocking Hook off his perch. Luckily, Bones is there to catch him. "Gotcha!"

"Quiet," whispers Smee. "I hear something."

"It's those puny pirates," says Hook. "Hide!"

Jake and his crew finally reach the tree, but Hook is gone. "Where could he be?" asks Jake.

Cubby checks his map. "Well, this path leads to Sailor Swamp."

"Maybe that's where we'll find Captain Hook," Izzy says.

"Right!" says Jake. "Then we can give him his hat back!"

But Hook's not at Sailor Swamp, either. "Let's look on the other side," says Cubby.

Izzy has an idea. "We can use this giant palm leaf as a boat!"

"Great," says Jake. "Come on!" The crew collects three more Gold Doubloons!

Captain Hook and Smee are following Jake. Hook doesn't think he needs a boat and sinks into the swamp!

Across the swamp, Jake and his crew find a beach. "Look," says Izzy. "The Jolly Roger."

"Ahoy, Captain Hook!" Izzy yells. "Are you there?" No one answers.

"I guess nobody's home!" says Skully.

Hook and Smee sneak up from behind. "Here I am!" shouts Hook. "Now give me my hat!"

"Here you go," says Jake. Hook reaches for the hat, then stops. "Wait! Is this a pirate trick?"

"It's no trick," Jake says. "We found your hat and we're returning it."

"It's the right thing to do," Izzy explains.

"No!" says Hook. "I won't take it."
"But, sir," says Smee. "Maybe it's not a trick."
"I know a trick when I see one!" says Hook.

"Aw, coconuts," Cubby says. "Now what?"

"I know," Izzy answers. "What if we just drop the hat on his head?"

"Yeah," says Jake. "Let's try it."

"A pinch of Pixie Dust is all we need!" Izzy says.

Hook doesn't even notice as Jake carefully sets the hat on his head.

"We did it!" Jake says.

"And, we got four more Gold Doubloons," says Cubby.

As the Never Land Pirates fly away, Smee tries to tell Hook that his hat has been returned.

"No, Mr. Smee, I will never take that hat back!" declares Hook.

"Oh, dear," sighs Smee.

Back on Pirate Island, Jake and the crew open the Team Treasure Chest. For solving Pirate Problems, they collected nine Gold Doubloons! "Yo ho, way to go!" shouts the crew.

"Ahoy! Thanks for your help, matey!"